EVERYTHING I NEED TO KNOW I LEARNED FROM

BRUCE SPRINGSTEEN

Wisdom From the Music and Musings of an American Dreamer

TREVOR COURNEEN

Bruce performs during the reopening night of *Springsteen on Broadway* at the St. James Theatre in New York City on June 26, 2021.

A TRIBUTE TO THE BOSS

WHETHER YOU'RE A New Jersey native, a blue-collar warrior born in the U.S.A. or simply a "tramp" running from the darkness on the edge of your town, Bruce Springsteen has a song for you. For decades, the Boss has used his music to put himself in the shoes of others, penning epic anthems that give a voice to the downtrodden, the romantics and the dreamers of the world. Even in the instances in which he's not speaking from direct experience—something he's gladly admitted to in recent years—Bruce is always speaking from the heart, proving himself to be one of the greatest empaths rock & roll has ever known. Whether he's electrifying a sold-out crowd alongside the E Street Band or stirring souls with his profoundly moving *Springsteen on Broadway* show, the Boss is, at his core, still one of us. And like the best of us, he believes that maybe if we all just keep working on this collective dream, we can make the world a better place. While he'd be the first to admit he doesn't have all the answers, Bruce's example is still one each of us can emulate, even if it only leads to being more true to ourselves.

Bruce takes a moment before performing with the E Street Band at Alex Cooley's Electric Ballroom in Atlanta, Georgia, on August 22, 1975.

Bruce performs
at Alex Cooley's
Electric Ballroom
in Atlanta, Georgia,
on August 21, 1975.

SHOW A LITTLE FAITH

Bruce's music reminds us that believing in a better tomorrow (or tonight) can keep your emotional engine running.

HOPE CAN BE a very powerful presence in our lives. When the chips are down, it can serve as a lifeline, an invisible getaway vehicle that arrives in the nick of time to help us steer through the wreckage. But according to Bruce, whose songs are filled with stories of characters facing serious struggles and unfavorable odds, sometimes hope requires a kick-start of its own. Even the most steadfast optimists in the world have to dig deep to find that faith when the going gets tough.

When Bruce explicitly says to "Show a little faith" in "Thunder Road," he sings the lyric with an added gusto that practically makes the words appear right before our eyes, highlighted and underlined in

Bruce on the
September 23,
2016, episode of
*The Late Show with
Stephen Colbert*.

big, bold type. While only uttered once within the nearly five-minute sweeping track, "Show a little faith" is the true crux of the song. Reflecting on the epic *Born to Run* opener in his autobiography, Bruce writes, "You are introduced to the album's central characters and its main proposition: do you want to take a chance?" The characters know they need to get out of town, but first they need to truly believe that they can find greener grass on the other side. Without faith, hope and all the summoned courage needed to "take a chance," those two lanes won't be able to take Mary and the narrator "anywhere."

Having hope is something we must actively engage with—we can't just count on it to be readily available to us at all times. As the Boss put it during a 2021 appearance on *The Late Show with Stephen Colbert*, "You have to be a fighting optimist." Life will constantly challenge your optimism, so hold tight to it. And once you've got a good grip on this fragile concept, don't be afraid to show it. There's a strong chance someone else needs to be reminded of its power.

Bruce perfor
Giants Stadium ir
Rutherford, New Je
on August 22,

NEVER UNDERESTIMATE THE VALUE OF ART

*"We learned more from a three-minute record, baby,
Than we ever learned in school"*

"NO SURRENDER"

MANY OF US experience art passively. There's nothing wrong with using music to drown out the rest of the world or half-watching a classic film while you clean the house. Just remember that when life gets dark, actively engaging with great art can help you find your way. Bruce has been on both sides of this equation, first finding strength and inspiration in the music of his youth and then later providing it to others through his own work. So many of the Boss's songs feel universally true because he recognizes one of the great responsibilities of being an artist: showing the audience they are not alone. And when that message is transmitted via rock & roll, it resonates beyond the rousing chorus or emotional key change. As any Bruce fan knows, some people can learn a lot by listening to music instead of lectures. But to learn, you still need to pay attention.

Bruce performs during the last show of the Born in the U.S.A. Tour on October 2, 1985, in Los Angeles, California.

GO THE DISTANCE FOR LOVE

The Boss's romantic anthems and tireless performances show how to express those warm, fuzzy feelings in an impactful way.

N "DRIVE ALL NIGHT" from 1980's *The River*, Bruce's narrator insists he'll travel "through the rain, the snow, the wind" to be reunited with the one he loves. He's even willing to pull an all-nighter behind the wheel just to buy his special someone a pair of shoes. While these lyrics may sound hyperbolic to a new listener, grand romantic gestures are ever-present in the Boss's catalog. His songs' narrators are willing to die in the streets in everlasting kisses, walk dark roads and thin, thin lines and return to that Kingstown bar (even if they probably shouldn't!). When love is the destination, no distance is too far.

The man behind these songs seems to feel the same way. Bruce has proven time and again just how far he'll go to express his love,

Bruce and Max Weinberg perform with the E Street Band at Citizens Bank Park in Philadelphia, Pennsylvania, on September 7, 2016.

particularly when it comes to his fans. On June 29, 1984, he embarked on what would grow into his lengthiest tour to date, the Born in the U.S.A. Tour. Ensuring everyone got the chance to experience the signature synths and anthemic choruses of his new hit album, Bruce extended the tour all the way to October 2, 1985, venturing beyond North America to make stops in Australia, Japan and various parts of Europe. More than three decades later, in 2016, the singer continued to show his fans just as much love as they've always shown him when he and the E Street Band broke their own performance record at a show in Philadelphia, clocking in at an incredible four hours and four minutes.

In the quiet moments at home, when he isn't surrounded by adoring fans, Bruce is still going the distance. In his autobiography *Born to Run*, the singer reveals he inherited some bad emotional habits from his father that initially hindered his relationship with his wife Patti. Fortunately, the Boss took the time and effort to distance himself from those old ways, as he writes, "For a couple of loners and musicians, we've made it pretty far." Love, in its many forms, can be an endurance test. But if you were to ask Bruce, he'd tell you it's always worth it.

Bruce opens for Stevie Wonder at Kutztown State College (now Kutztown University of Pennsylvania) on March 29, 1973.

"Mama always told me not to look into the sights of the sun Whoa, but mama, that's where the fun is"

"BLINDED BY THE LIGHT"

• • •

Whether it's the sun or the spotlight, the young poet spouting endless rhymes in "Blinded by the Light" is dying to be engulfed in it. In this introductory track, Bruce made himself known as a man ready to take risks in order to get the most out of life. Sometimes you have to be bold and daring to get the fulfillment you seek.

Bruce takes a bow on the opening night of *Springsteen on Broadway* at the Walter Kerr Theatre in New York City on October 12, 2017.

FIND THE MAGIC IN THE MUNDANE

Many of Bruce's songs highlight how the ordinary aspects of life are what make it extraordinary.

N THE OPENING MOMENTS of his spectacular *Springsteen on Broadway* show, Bruce takes a wrecking ball to the fourth wall. Standing before a sold-out Walter Kerr Theatre, night after night, the singer would explain the expectations of his job: "These are fans who are waiting for you to pull something out of your hat, out of thin air, something out of this world…" But the real magic trick in play here, as the Boss puts it, is his ability to simply provide "proof of life."

The problem, as most know too well, is that real life can be pretty boring. It's natural to get tired of toiling away on the job or feel like you're stuck in a time loop repeating the same routine day after day (in another meta moment of *Springsteen on Broadway*, Bruce jokes about

Patti Scialfa and Bruce during *Springsteen on Broadway* at the Walter Kerr Theatre in New York City on October 12, 2017.

this very feeling: "I've never worked five days a week until right now—I don't like it!"). But when we hear our own struggles conveyed through song, the perception starts to change. Whether it's the motivational spirit of "Night" or the exuberant pride of "Working on the Highway," music can help us see the joy in what we do.

This perceived "magic" is just the inverse of an old expression—it's art imitating life. Bruce has never concocted a song by literally conjuring the spirits of rock & roll, as much as it may seem that way sometimes. He's simply been taking what he sees, no matter how gray and gloomy it may appear, and putting it through a kaleidoscopic lens (more on this on pg. 94). And you can do the same. If you take a closer, more imaginative look at all the seemingly dull aspects of your day-to-day life, you might see a glimmer of magic—or at least the potential for it.

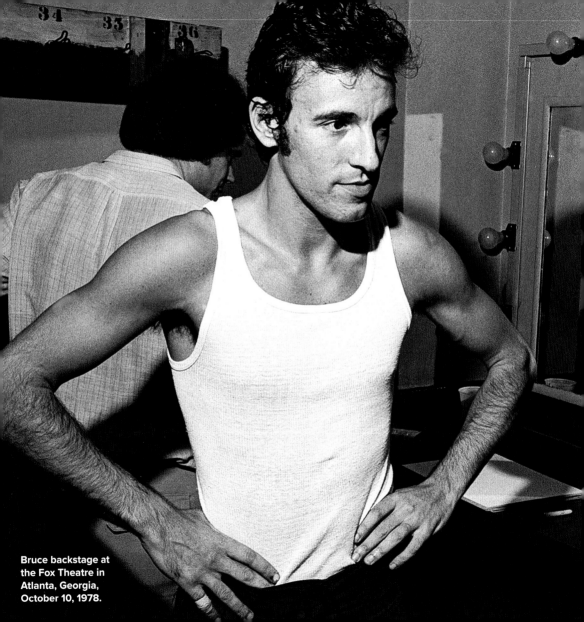

Bruce backstage at the Fox Theatre in Atlanta, Georgia, October 10, 1978.

TAKE CONTROL OF YOUR DESTINY

"You spend your life waiting for a moment that just don't come / Well don't waste your time waiting."

"BADLANDS"

RUCE'S CLASSIC 1978 album *Darkness on the Edge of Town* contains some of the grittiest, hardest truths he's ever told in his music, and it all begins with the spirited opening track "Badlands." A logical follow-up to the themes found on *Born to Run*, "Badlands" is told from the perspective of a narrator who's seen enough heartache and hardship to know you can't just leave your life in the hands of fate and trust everything will work out. "Talk about a dream, try to make it real," the Boss sings as the song builds toward its explosive first chorus. It's a rousing reminder that if you want to reach the major milestones, you'll have to put in a lot of work and weather a few storms along the way. You can't just talk about a dream. You have to try.

Bruce greets his fans during a concert, c. 1975.

WE WERE BORN TO RUN

That burning desire to go out and seek something greater than your default surroundings—a common theme found throughout Bruce's music—is essential for self-discovery.

WHETHER OR NOT you actually consider yourself a "tramp," you likely feel very much a part of the "we" in the lyric "we were born to run." Though Bruce's narrator is technically addressing his muse Wendy in the song, the Boss might as well be speaking directly to his fan base. "Born to Run" stands tall as one of Bruce's most beloved and best-known songs and is often the gateway track that reels in new fans—not just because it's a timeless classic, but because of the feeling of inclusivity it provides. When the E Street Band launches into the song live, the house lights come on, transforming an arena full of like-minded music lovers into a congregation singing the signature hymn of their rock & roll church.

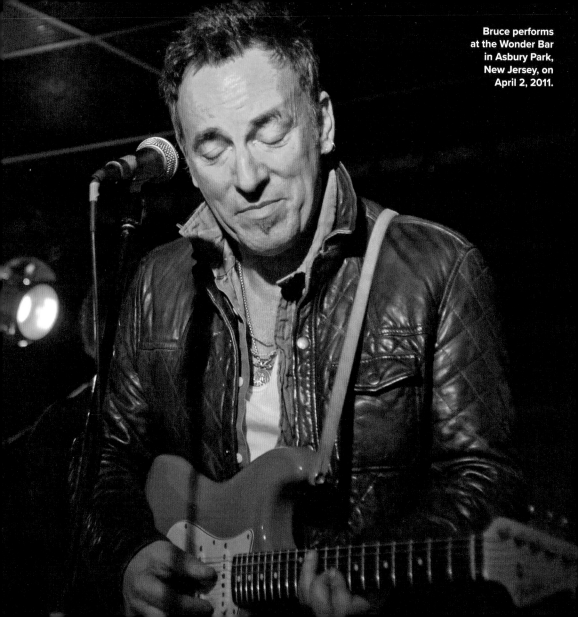

Bruce performs at the Wonder Bar in Asbury Park, New Jersey, on April 2, 2011.

We all feel the urge to run from time to time, whether it's toward something or away (or often, both). This feeling is not only natural but essential. But what it means to "run" truly depends on your situation (as Bruce himself has joked, he did all that "running" just to end up settling down about 10 minutes from where he grew up). What's truly important is the process of exploration and self-discovery, neither of which requires you to actually travel some great distance. You can run by quitting your job in order to go to college and explore different career options. You can run by breaking off a relationship you've deemed unhealthy in favor of taking time to focus on your own needs and wants. Whatever it may be, you just have to do it. Standing still, whether you're doing it literally or figuratively, is bound to stunt your growth as a person. So just get going—someday, even if you don't know when, you're gonna get to that place where you really wanna go.

Bruce and his wife Patti Scialfa with their daughter Jessica Springsteen at the Royal Windsor Horse Show in Berkshire, England, May 14, 2011.

YOU CAN BE THE BOSS
WITHOUT GRINDING 24/7

"I love my job. Great way to make a living, no way to live."

THE LATE SHOW WITH STEPHEN COLBERT, 2021

THE MOST PASSIONATE workaholics often come to a crossroads: either establish a firm barrier between personal and professional life or allow work to eclipse everything else until it's all that they are. Unfortunately, there's an important fact many of these ambitious individuals don't understand: this crossroads is imaginary. For proof, look no further than Bruce Springsteen.

On *The Late Show with Stephen Colbert* in 2021, Bruce told the host, "It can be very, very dangerous to you mentally, physically, [if you're] not cleaving between your work life and your family life, your home life. You've got to make some very clear boundaries and distinctions if you want to live a full life in both of those areas." Considering he's a rock & roll icon and a beloved husband, father and grandfather, Bruce speaks from experience. It may take time to figure out, but once you learn to balance work and home life, you're bound to enjoy both a lot more.

Bruce sits at the wheel of a Cadillac convertible c. 1987.

"You've got to learn to live with what you can't rise above"

"TUNNEL OF LOVE"

• • •

As mighty as he may seem to some of his most die-hard admirers, Bruce is, like the rest of us, only human. For evidence, look no further than the title track from his "divorce album," 1987's *Tunnel of Love*, in which he offers his method for navigating the types of struggles we all wish would just disappear. If you can't escape certain hardships, figure out how to power through them.

BRUCE SPRINGSTEEN

The "Dancing in the Dark" 12-inch single, which was released on May 9, 1984.

DANCING IN THE DARK

DANCE IN THE DARK

One of Bruce's biggest hits is a reminder to just keep moving to the beat, even when it feels like your world is falling apart.

WITH A CAREER spanning more than half a century, Bruce has always managed to stay razor-sharp as a songwriter. The Boss is revered not just for making ear-pleasing music but for crafting songs that subvert expectations and carry embedded messages deeper than their surface level might suggest. Sometimes, the tunes are so toe-tappingly catchy that the meaning gets a little lost in translation (see pg. 40). In "Dancing in the Dark," Bruce manages to express everything from feelings of isolation and loneliness to the woes of aging all while making his listeners get up and move to the sounds of '80s pop perfection. It's an example of his oft-discussed "magic," but it's a trick we can all learn with a little practice.

Bruce dances with Courteney Cox during the filming of the "Dancing in the Dark" music video, which was filmed in St. Paul, Minnesota.

"Dancing in the Dark" came about largely because Bruce needed a surefire radio hit for his upcoming album, 1984's *Born in the U.S.A.* The demand for such a song put a lot of pressure on the Boss and understandably stirred up some lingering frustration in both his personal and professional life. But that frustration turned out to be the spark that started the fire, as Bruce wound up with a song that allows audiences to gleefully sing along to sentiments they've likely felt themselves, such as "Wanna change my clothes, my hair, my face." And the joyful feeling of reciting those brooding lyrics isn't just thanks to the uplifting melody—it's because the Boss pairs the dark introspection with lines like "There's a joke here somewhere and it's on me." As the song goes on, he starts to laugh at himself, something we all could stand to do on occasion. It's circumstantial, of course, but sometimes there's dark humor—or at least a danceable beat—to be found in rough patches.

The Boss and his wife Patti Scialfa at Sam's Restaurant in New York City on May 9, 1992.

OUR STRUGGLES MAKE US HUMAN

"So you been broken and you been hurt
Show me somebody who ain't"

"HUMAN TOUCH"

ET'S FACE IT: many of life's most valuable lessons come from the not-so-good times. The aftermath of a tough period is a chance to pick up the pieces and notice what went wrong, as well as what you can do differently next time. But as Bruce points out in "Human Touch," heartache is far from unique—and it shouldn't be used as an excuse or a measuring stick against others.

In this track from his 1992 album of the same name, Bruce's narrator is a straight shooter talking to a lover. He's not trying to deny the possibility of more heartbreak ("You can't shut off the risk and pain"), but he's also not about to let it derail their relationship. As for the times they've seemingly both been burned in the past, the narrator views those experiences as a uniting factor, particularly in the chorus lyric, "I just want someone to talk to/ And a little of that human touch." If we bond over bad times, there's a chance we can forge a real connection that leads to a lot of good.

Clarence Clemons and Bruce perform at Rupp Arena in Lexington, Kentucky, on December 12, 1984.

A CLEAR MESSAGE CAN STILL BE MISUNDERSTOOD

Ever since its release, "Born in the U.S.A." has been famously misunderstood by campaigning politicians, proving that even the loudest statements can fall on deaf ears.

A TRUE SPRINGSTEEN FAN (affectionately known as a "Bruce Tramp" in some circles) can attest that while the Boss is a shining symbol of Americana, the patriotism found in his music does not come without criticism (more on this on pg. 50). Still, ever since 1984 when *Born in the U.S.A.* shifted Bruce's aesthetic to red and white stripes and blue-collar clothes, many casual listeners have misunderstood the message behind the album's title track. This persistent misconception is a reminder of a frustrating scenario we all face from time to time: Even when you think you're speaking clearly, you can still be misunderstood.

Among those who have likely never listened to the lyrics of "Born in

Bruce performs during
The Concert for Valor
at the National Mall in
Washington, D.C., on
November 11, 2014.

the U.S.A.," politicians are the most glaring example. For four decades now, rather than recognizing it as a protest song against the country's well-documented mistreatment of Vietnam veterans, elected officials have been using the song as a simplistic, fist-pumping "America is #1!" anthem. The cruel irony began following the song's release, after former President Ronald Reagan attempted to use it during his reelection campaign (meanwhile in his first term, he cut millions of dollars from veterans benefits). Most recently, former President Donald Trump also failed to get the memo as the song frequently played at his rallies. The Boss has had quite a bit to say about Trump, whose actions he once called "outrageously anti-American, so totally buffoonish and so stupid and so anti-freedom of speech."

There's plenty to be learned from both sides here. You can still love your country while protesting its involvement in war. You have to look (and listen) beyond what's on the surface level. And if you're the one trying to spread a message, sometimes you have to accept that some people only hear what they want to hear.

Bruce performs in the 2019 *Western Stars* documentary.

"A time comes when you
need to stop waiting for
the man you want to become
and start being the
man you want to be."

BRUCE SPRINGSTEEN

THE PEOPLE IN POWER DON'T SPEAK FOR EVERYONE

Bruce has chosen to be a voice for the voiceless on many occasions.

A S SOMEONE WHO has always stood up for society's underdogs, Bruce has long understood that people are not defined by the politics of the place in which they live. In 2004, the Boss tried to amplify as many American voices as possible when he embarked on the Vote for Change Tour, which sought to earn votes for John Kerry in the presidential election against incumbent George W. Bush. Joined by fellow rock legends including Neil Young, R.E.M. and Pearl Jam, Bruce made a lasting impact on songwriter Conor Oberst, whose band Bright Eyes also performed on the tour. Shortly after Bush was reelected, Oberst was dreading a scheduled press trip to Europe. "That was at the height of the Europeans hating

Bruce performs during a campaign rally for Hillary Clinton in Philadelphia, Pennsylvania, on November 7, 2016.

Bush and the Iraq War," Oberst told Marc Maron on the *WTF* podcast. "And I was like, 'Man, I'm gonna go and this is all they're gonna want to talk about.'" But Bruce, sensing Oberst might need a patriotic pep talk, called the young songwriter just as he was about to board the plane. "He's like, 'Conor, you go over there and tell 'em there's half of us who don't believe in this—there's a real America over here and we're gonna fight really hard.'"

Twelve years later, the Boss would again stand up for the "real America" when a controversial law in North Carolina sparked a national conversation. Known as HB2, the law required transgender people to only use public bathrooms corresponding with the sex they were assigned at birth. Bruce, like numerous other performers at the time, responded by canceling his shows in the Tar Heel State. Addressing the decision in a statement, he said, "I feel that this is a time for me and the band to show solidarity with those freedom fighters." If you don't identify with the people in power, speak up. Your voice can make a difference in someone else's life. You'll likely hear it echoing back when you need it, too.

Bruce performs in Los Angeles, California, c. 1984.

HOLD YOUR COUNTRY
TO A HIGHER STANDARD

"There is a real patriotism underneath the best of my music, but it is a critical, questioning and often angry patriotism."

THE GUARDIAN, 2012

I N A *ROLLING STONE* interview in 1984, the same year *Born in the U.S.A.* entered the world, Bruce reflected, "I think people got a need to feel good about the country they live in. But what's happening, I think, is that that need—which is a good thing—is gettin' manipulated and exploited." Too often, people who talk about the ways their country could improve are deemed "unpatriotic"—but the opposite is true. As Bruce told *The Guardian*, there is a "real patriotism" in his music, and the key word here is "real." This nuance has been on display since the mid-'80s when he performed before an Old Glory backdrop every night, singing about his dreams of a more united and fair America.

Despite his criticisms, it's clear that the Boss still believes in the promise of the United States. You can love your country while still pointing out its flaws. In fact, the former should inform the latter.

Bruce receives the Presidential Medal of Freedom from President Barack Obama during a ceremony at the White House on November 22, 2016.

The vinyl record cover art for
Bruce's 1973 debut album,
Greetings from Asbury Park, N.J.

SELFLESSNESS HELPS OTHERS SUCCEED...

It's natural to want recognition for your work, but Bruce has shown that sometimes it's best to share the fruits of your labor.

WHEN BRUCE RELEASED *Greetings from Asbury Park, N.J.* in 1973, he was young, hungry and aiming to make a name for himself. The album's loquacious opening track is essentially his mission statement to the world, as he later revealed on *VH1 Storytellers*: "I wanted to get blinded by the light, I wanted to do things I hadn't done and see things I hadn't seen." And while he would absolutely go on to do just that, it wasn't exactly thanks to "Blinded by the Light." A few years later in 1976, the song's association with the Boss would begin to fade when a new version by Manfred Mann took over the airwaves. Eventually, the English rock group's cover went to No. 1 in the United States—a feat Bruce has still

Bruce and Patti Smith perform at a screening of the documentary *Horses: Patti Smith and Her Band* during the 2018 Tribeca Film Festival in New York City on April 23, 2018.

never achieved. But he welcomed his work seeing success in the hands of others, telling the *VH1 Storytellers* audience with a glint of humor, "This song is my only number one song... and it wasn't done by me, it was done by Manfred Mann, which I appreciate."

The following year in 1977, Bruce would graciously entrust another creation to a songwriter on the rise, Patti Smith. After recording "Because the Night" during sessions for *Darkness on the Edge of Town*, the singer felt the track didn't fit within the themes of the album. Smith was recording her album *Easter* at the same studio at the time, and after a conversation with producer Jimmy Iovine, the Boss was more than happy to give "Because the Night" to the woman now known as the "punk poet laureate." Smith's rendition would become one of her biggest hits, and the two legends got to share a full-circle moment when they performed the song together at the 25th anniversary Rock & Roll Hall of Fame ceremony.

A job well done warrants great pride, but a different type of pride develops when you're able to share the spotlight. Seeing others thrive and knowing you had a hand in helping them do so is an evergreen joy.

BRUCE SPRINGSTEEN

HUNGRY HEART

b/w **HELD UP WITHOUT A GUN**

The cover art for the "Hungry Heart" single, which features Bruce on the boardwalk in Asbury Park, New Jersey.

...BUT TAKE CREDIT WHERE IT'S DUE

The story behind the Boss's classic track "Hungry Heart" proves you can pat yourself on the back without breaking your spine.

HUMILITY IS A virtue, and Bruce has it in spades. For decades, the singer has proven unfazed by the fact that many don't recognize him as the songwriter behind hits such as "Blinded by the Light" and "Because the Night." Of course, he also knows when he's holding a winning hand, and there's plenty to learn from one instance in which the rock icon opted to bask in the glory.

"Hungry Heart" is one of Bruce's biggest radio hits (reaching number 5 on the Billboard Hot 100 in 1980) and one of his most crowd-pleasing concert staples (the Boss frequently allows his audience to sing the entire first verse without him). However, the songwriter's early generosity with his work almost cost him one of the most beloved

The Boss crowd surfs during a show in Baltimore, Maryland, on November 20, 2009.

classics in his catalog. As Bruce told Jimmy Fallon on *The Tonight Show* in 2015, he initially wrote the song—coincidentally about a man who takes a "wrong turn" in his life—with the intention of giving it to the Ramones. The Boss and the legendary punk group crossed paths after a show in Asbury Park one night, and Bruce, being a fan, decided to pen something for them. But after hearing the obvious potential of "Hungry Heart," as legend goes, the Boss's manager Jon Landau and Joey Ramone both encouraged him to keep it for himself.

Today, when the E Street Band launches into "Hungry Heart" in concert, Bruce often takes the opportunity to crowd surf, allowing himself to be lifted up by a sea of fans singing every lyric at the top of their lungs. Don't be afraid to accept acclaim for your accomplishments. If you allow yourself to enjoy what you've achieved, you're likely to keep discovering ways to repeat that success.

"Walk tall
Or baby, don't walk at all"

"NEW YORK CITY SERENADE"

• • •

While set in the City That Never Sleeps, this lyric from *The Wild, the Innocent & the E Street Shuffle* closer "New York City Serenade" is sage wisdom for anyone, anywhere. Bruce has never phoned in a single moment of his career, proving that anything worth doing deserves 100 percent effort. Otherwise, don't even bother.

5 LPs

BRUCE SPRINGSTEEN
& THE E STREET BAND
LIVE/1975-85

Bruce's *Live 1975-85*
album, which features the
September 30, 1985, performance
of "The River" in Los Angeles.

FORGIVENESS IS PAINFUL BUT POWERFUL

Bruce spent his younger years learning that good intentions can hide behind hurtful actions.

RUCE'S DIFFICULT RELATIONSHIP with his father has been at the forefront of his personal and professional life many times over the years (more on this on pg. 140). But despite detailing his father's destructive ways and how he became a "terrifying, all-engulfing presence" when he drank, Bruce has always managed to see the good in his old man, too. Just a couple of lines after giving that description in *Born to Run*, the Boss mentions "the goodness and kindness in his heart, of which there was plenty."

While introducing a performance of "The River" during a tour stop in Los Angeles on September 30, 1985, the singer told a story that perfectly encapsulates the dichotomy that existed within Douglas Springsteen. When Bruce was a long-haired, meandering musician in his late teens, he and his father fought so frequently that Bruce would try to be out of the house as much as possible. On the rare nights they

Bruce looks on as his son, Sam Springsteen, shakes hands with then-Senator Barack Obama at a presidential campaign rally in Cleveland, Ohio, on November 2, 2008.

did cross paths, the Springsteen patriarch would sit his son down and lay into him, saying, "When the Army gets you, they're gonna make a man out of you." The threat carried real weight—at the time, plenty of young men from Bruce's neighborhood were going to Vietnam, including the drummer from his first band. "A lot of guys went, and a lot of guys didn't come back," the Boss told the crowd. Soon enough, Bruce got his draft notice—but ultimately failed the physical. When he returned home three days later and broke the news, his father simply said, "That's good."

Years later, after the Boss's career had skyrocketed and he was about to become a father himself, an unexpected visitor showed up at his doorstep. "Bruce, you've been very good to us," his father began after sitting down inside, "And I wasn't very good to you." Grateful to receive any acknowledgment of their painful past, Bruce told his father, "You did the best you could."

You might not be as forgiving as Bruce, and that's OK. Everyone's pain is their own to process. The decision to rebuild or repair a relationship with someone who hurt you is ultimately yours, so be sure you're putting your own best interest first.

Bruce and the E Street Band, c. 1984. From left: Garry Tallent, Bruce Springsteen, Nils Lofgren, Danny Federici, Clarence Clemons, Roy Bittan and Max Weinberg.

Bob Dylan and Bruce perform at the Rock & Roll Hall of Fame in Cleveland, Ohio, on September 2, 1995.

BE AN INDIVIDUAL

*"I hid in the clouded wrath of the crowd
But when they said, 'Sit down,' I stood up"*

"GROWING UP"

WHEN YOU WANT to make a meaningful first impression, it's natural to base your strategy on the proven success of someone else. There's nothing wrong with borrowing bits and pieces from others, regardless of what you're setting out to achieve—many of the greatest works of art take inspiration from what came before. But no matter whom you choose to model yourself after, it's crucial to make sure your own voice remains the loudest, even if you're taking some cues from someone as prolific as Bruce Springsteen. Or, in Bruce's case, Bob Dylan.

On his debut album *Greetings from Asbury Park, N.J.*, Bruce's standout talent is clear across all nine energizing tracks. But thanks to his propensity for poetic lyrics spanning multiple verses per song, the Boss was likened to another legend in the making. "Once the record was released, I heard all the Dylan comparisons," he wrote in 2016's *Born to Run*, "so I steered away from it." If you're afraid of getting lost in the crowd, be the one who defiantly stands up to stand out.

BRUCE
SPRINGSTEEN

BORN TO RUN

Bruce displays his King's
Court Elvis Presley Fan Club
of NYC pin on his guitar
strap on the cover of his
1975 album *Born to Run*.

MISCHIEF CAN BE MEANINGFUL

A formative moment in Bruce's life proves there's good fun to be had in doing the wrong thing for the right reasons.

O N APRIL 29, 1976, the Boss was continuing to live his dream while playing a show in Memphis, Tennessee. But once his performing duties were done that night, Bruce let his own rock & roll fandom take over when he paid a spontaneous visit to Elvis Presley's Graceland. Naturally, viewing his hero's home from afar wasn't quite enough in the thrilling moment. "I looked at Steve [Van Zandt] and said, 'Steve, I'm going in,'" Bruce recalled on *The Graham Norton Show* in 2019. "When's the opportunity going to come again?" And so, believing he was seizing a once-in-a-lifetime moment, Bruce jumped the wall and ran up the hill to the legendary mansion. When he got to the door, however, the Boss was not greeted by the King, but

Steven Van Zandt and Bruce at WQXI Radio in Atlanta, Georgia, on March 27, 1976.

rather a security guard who kindly escorted him off the property. The risks of being arrested, injured or profoundly embarrassed were of no concern to Bruce, who clearly felt any such outcome was well worth the chance to meet Elvis.

Forty years after his infamous Graceland visit, the Boss appeared on *The Late Show with Stephen Colbert*, which films in a very significant venue: the Ed Sullivan Theater. Sitting on the same stage where the King of Rock & Roll played "Hound Dog" on *The Ed Sullivan Show* and inspired a 7-year-old kid in Freehold, New Jersey, to pick up a guitar for the first time, Bruce and Colbert watched a clip of the iconic performance. With a big smile on his face, the Boss told the host, "That's why I got here."

Today, when fans get a little too close to his own home, Bruce can't get too upset as he remembers exactly how it feels to be overcome with that kind of excitement. Even if you're someone who always strives to walk the straight and narrow, try to keep your mind open to the idea of dabbling in harmless mischief once in a while. You might just make a memory that will last a lifetime.

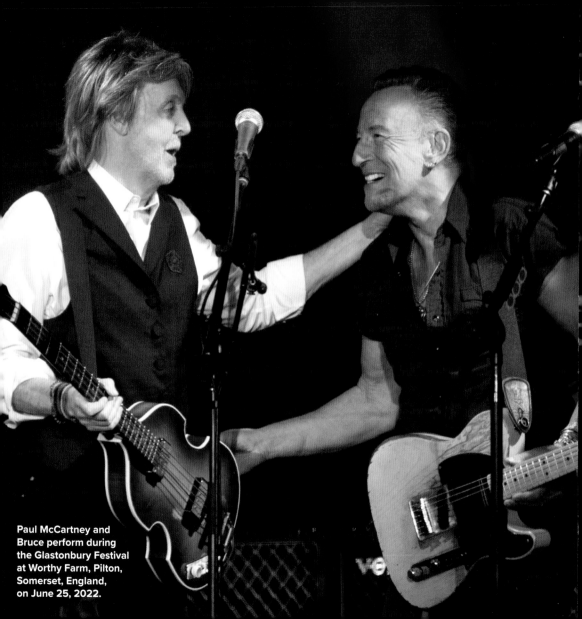

Paul McCartney and Bruce perform during the Glastonbury Festival at Worthy Farm, Pilton, Somerset, England, on June 25, 2022.

"The great challenge of
adulthood is holding on
to your idealism after
you lose your innocence."

BRUCE SPRINGSTEEN

FLY BLIND FROM TIME TO TIME

If you lack the knowledge needed to do something, you can occasionally make up for it with sheer confidence.

N A HIGHLY entertaining tale that precedes "The Promised Land" in *Springsteen on Broadway*, Bruce opens up about being in his 20s before he learned to drive. "The man who would very, very shortly write 'Racing in the Street,'" he adds, drawing big laughs. The Boss's high-pressure debut behind the wheel reveals a lesson that might sound scary on paper: sometimes you just have to give it your best shot, even if you have no clue what you're doing.

Desperate to get out of the confines of New Jersey to have a real chance at being discovered, Bruce and his burgeoning band scraped together enough cash to drive thousands of miles across the country for a New Year's Eve gig in Big Sur, California. The crew had two vehicles: Danny Federici's station wagon, complete with a mattress in the back in lieu of hotel beds, and new manager Carl "Tinker" West's 1940s flatbed, which would haul the gear. With only three days to get there, there was

Bruce performs with the E Street Band in Paris, France, on July 4, 2012.

no time to stop for anything but gas, which meant everyone needed to take the wheel for long shifts. But somewhere in Nashville, Bruce and Tinker got separated from the station wagon full of drivers—"When you lose someone in a world without the cellular phone," the Boss reminds the audience, "oh, they're fuckin' lost." Forced to forge ahead, Tinker continued on until his eyes told him it was time for Bruce to take the driver's seat. After struggling to understand manual transmission, the young musician found a groove: "I was fine in second, third and fourth [gear] and I could keep it in between the lines as long as I didn't have to stop or go near first gear." Still, Bruce's shift didn't allow Tinker to catch any Z's. As the Boss puts it, "He's awake anyway, because a guy who can't drive is driving!"

In the decades since, Bruce has continued to fly blind on occasion—albeit in a much safer sense. The rock icon has a longstanding tradition of taking cover requests during concerts by selecting signs held up by fans in the crowd. Sometimes, the E Street Band ends up playing a song together for the first time, right then and there in front of thousands of onlookers. The results may vary, but certain situations call for figuring things out as you go.

BRUCE SPRINGSTEEN

THE RIVER

Bruce's 1980 album *The River*.

DREAM BIG,
BUT BE PREPARED FOR SETBACKS

"Is a dream a lie when it don't come true? / Or is it something worse?"

"THE RIVER"

EVERYONE DREAMS EVERY night of their lives, and while some dreams aren't even remembered in the morning, others can never be forgotten. The latter type can inspire incredible real-world results, but they can also set you up for severe disappointment if you're not careful.

Dreams are the driving force behind much of Bruce's music, from the ambitions of his characters to his vision of a more united society. But in the title track from 1980's *The River*, Bruce's narrator poses the above question, which lingers like a dark cloud. In contrast to the optimism of "Thunder Road" or "Born to Run," "The River" is told from the perspective of someone who feels betrayed by his dreams. On his 19th birthday, with an unplanned baby on the way, he gets "a union card and a wedding coat." Sometimes, life disagrees with your best-laid plans. You have to be prepared to dust yourself off and adapt as best you can.

Patti Scialfa and Bruce perform during *Jersey 4 Jersey*, a broadcast fundraiser to fight COVID-19's impact on New Jersey, on April 22, 2020.

BE ABSOLUTELY CERTAIN THERE ARE NO ABSOLUTES

Bruce believes strength of character is fueled by the ability to balance opposing ideas.

THE BOSS MAY appear to be the coolest, most confident artist to ever grace a stage, but his willingness to be wide open about his struggles and shortcomings over the years has painted a much more well-rounded portrait of the man behind the music (more on this on pg. 102). And according to the singer himself, the ability to simultaneously be an unshakable rock star and a vulnerable everyman is one of the secrets to his success.

Delivering a keynote address at the 2012 South by Southwest festival, Bruce laid out this philosophy in amusing terms. Standing before a crowd of young musicians on the rise, the Boss encouraged the artists to believe in their own greatness—as long as they were also willing to take

Bruce and the E Street Band

themselves down a peg or two. "Don't take yourself too seriously. Take yourself as seriously as death itself," he offered. "Don't worry. Worry your ass off. Have iron-clad confidence, but doubt. It keeps you alive and alert! Believe you are the baddest ass in town—and you suck! It keeps you honest. Be able to keep two completely contradictory ideas alive and well inside of your heart and head at all times. If it doesn't drive you crazy, it will make you strong." At the end of the speech, the icon suggested a dichotomy he's worked hard to perfect (see pg. 28), telling the crowd, "When you walk on stage tonight to bring the noise, treat it like it's all we have—and then remember it's only rock & roll."

You can't expect to be 100 percent unfailingly brave, confident, enthusiastic or whatever it may be. Contradictory feelings—fear, doubt, apathy—are bound to creep in. You won't always be able to fight them off, and sometimes you shouldn't. There's nuance to be discovered when black-and-white ideas clash into gray—which is often where you'll find the closest thing to the truth.

The Boss performs in concert c. 1988.

LIFE ISN'T JUST PEAKS AND VALLEYS

"Pessimism and optimism are slammed up against each other in my records, the tension between them is where it's all at; it's what lights the fire."

THE GUARDIAN, 2012

WE'VE ALL BEEN guilty of only seeing things in black and white (pg. 86), such as having "the worst week ever" and then remedying it with "the best weekend of all time." Believing the tension between such extremes is what "lights the fire," the Boss has spent his career crafting an ongoing war between pessimism and optimism. While *Born to Run* is a fantastical dream full of hope, *Darkness on the Edge of Town* is the harsh reality of waking up and facing the circumstances you're still stuck in. Often, the tension exists within the same album. *The River*'s title track is a gloomy tale of broken dreams (see pg. 82), but it's pitted against the likes of "Crush on You." Though many of his songs are works of fiction, Bruce's truthful depictions of the human experience remind us that much of life takes place somewhere in between the best and worst of times.

"Well let there be sunlight,
let there be rain
Let my broken heart love again"

"SHERRY DARLING"

• • •

One of the standout tracks from *The River* thanks to its house party jubilance,
"Sherry Darling" welcomes not only the good times but also the tough times.
You need the occasional rain to better appreciate the sunlight, much like having
a previously broken heart makes falling in love again feel all the better.

Bruce prepares in his dressing room at the Asbury Park Convention Hall on March 23, 2009.

AMPLIFY THE GIFTS YOU'RE GIVEN

Bruce's success isn't merely the result of his talent but rather the masterful way in which he wields it.

N HIS AUTOBIOGRAPHY *Born to Run*, the Boss makes a major confession right off the bat: "I come from a boardwalk town where everything is tinged with a bit of fraud. So am I." Soon after the book's release, Bruce would reiterate that statement in the opening moments of *Springsteen on Broadway*, followed by an added kicker. "Standing before you is a man who has become wildly and absurdly successful writing about something of which he has had…absolutely no personal experience," the singer says, drawing big laughs as he references the fact that he's never worked a blue-collar job. "I made it all up. That's how good I am!"

Even with his unmatched charisma, his powerful voice and his skill for

Bruce greets fans during a concert at the Times-Union Center in Albany, New York, on February 8, 2016.

making a guitar "talk," Bruce's greatest gift has always been his ability to tell a story. His music is populated with fleshed-out characters—Wendy, Mary, Rosalita, Outlaw Pete, to name a few—and settings that drive the plot just as much as any living, breathing thing—Asbury Park, New York City, the Utah desert, Kingstown and many more. When it came time to write his autobiography, the Boss proved his ability to captivate didn't even require musical accompaniment. He even figured out a way to take it to the next level with *Springsteen on Broadway*, a show that puts a particularly bright spotlight on his most awe-inspiring strengths: storytelling, songwriting and performing.

Whether operating in fact or fiction, Bruce has an incredible knack for using his talent to connect with the masses. "That's what artists do," he said on *The Late Show with Stephen Colbert* in 2016. "They lie in service of the truth." You might be an absolute natural at what you do, but if you're not doing it wisely, you run the risk of minimizing your potential. The trick is to hone what you're given and learn how to use it as effectively as possible.

The Boss gives his all during a performance in Los Angeles, California, c. 1979.

ESTABLISH A SANCTUARY

"Let's just do the show. I'm safe there, I know what's going on, I know what's expected of me, I have no problem busting my ass to deliver it."

WTF WITH MARC MARON, 2017

FROM THE PAINFUL aftereffects of his childhood to his recent battle with depression, Bruce is living proof that not all obstacles can be outgrown. So, when he sat down to chat with Marc Maron on the comedian's *WTF* podcast in 2017, it was no surprise to learn he considers his concerts a cleansing escape from the surrounding noise. "At the end of the evening, I can go home and put my head to sleep on my pillow in a short moment of peace," the singer said.

On stage, Bruce appears equipped to shut out anything he's dealing with via the power of rock & roll and community. And as any fan knows, he's never in a rush to leave this sanctuary. Revisiting this concept with Howard Stern in 2022, Bruce referred to his marathon-like performances as a "purification ritual." You may not have the luxury of walking into a room full of thousands of people who adore you, but there's a good chance you do have a safe space or hobby that reliably recharges your batteries. Don't deny yourself a retreat when you need it.

Bruce backstage at the
Asbury Park Convention Hall
on March 23, 2009.

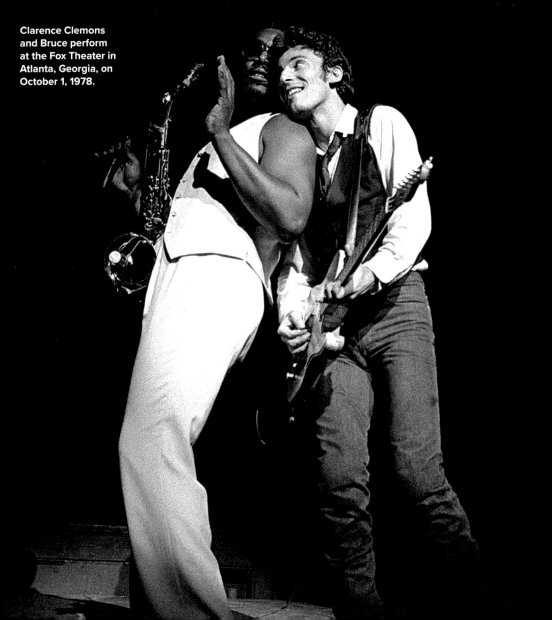

Clarence Clemons and Bruce perform at the Fox Theater in Atlanta, Georgia, on October 1, 1978.

WEAR EMOTIONS ON YOUR SLEEVE

**As Bruce would no doubt profess,
there are plenty of benefits to baring your soul.**

B RUCE HAS ALWAYS displayed a masculinity that isn't typically paired with vulnerability—but then again, the Boss is far from typical. He has long understood the importance of wearing his heart on his sleeve (even when he's not wearing sleeves, e.g., the Born in the U.S.A. Tour).

As the legend told NPR in 2016, "If you just looked at the outside, it's pretty alpha-male, which is a little ironic, because that was personally never exactly really me." From a young age, Bruce has been a stark contrast to the types of emotionally closed-off men he grew up around, writing in his autobiography *Born to Run*, "[I had] a gentleness, a timidity, shyness and a dreamy insecurity," all of which he "wore on the outside." Even when his stage persona became an effort to emulate his dismissive father in the 1980s (more on pg. 143), the Boss maintained his expressive ways. At a given show, the singer could be seen running

Bruce at his home in
Colts Neck, New Jersey,
on September 26, 2019.

into the embracing arms of Clarence Clemons or stealing a smooch from the Big Man's lips while sharing a mic. With these very public displays of affection, Bruce became what a 2020 feature on *InsideHook* dubbed "an icon of non-toxic masculinity."

While he excelled at showing love for others, the rock legend had to fight an uphill battle before he could be honest with himself about the darker feelings he harbored. In a 2018 interview with *Esquire*, Bruce opened up about his mental health struggles and the defense mechanisms he used, saying, "I relied on them wrongly to isolate myself, seal my alienation, cut me off from life, control others, and contain my emotions to a damaging degree. Now the bill collector is knocking, and his payment will be in tears." Simply admitting to that struggle was a massive step forward, and thanks to his willingness to detail his battles with depression in his autobiography, Bruce undoubtedly inspired others to release some of their most closely guarded feelings.

For many folks, being openly emotional is much more easily said than done. But when you finally do communicate exactly how you feel, you provide yourself a freedom no one else can offer.

Patti Scialfa and Bruce with then-Senator Barack Obama and Michelle Obama at a campaign rally in Cleveland, Ohio, on November 2, 2008.

PAIN BECOMES STRENGTH OVER TIME

"You have to turn your ghosts into ancestors. Ghosts haunt you, ancestors walk alongside you."

RENEGADES: BORN IN THE USA PODCAST

NO ONE REACHES adulthood completely unscathed. But as Bruce has underscored for more than five decades, the passage of time can allow painful memories to evolve into sources of strength.

On an episode of their podcast *Renegades: Born in the USA*, the Boss and Barack Obama spoke about "carrying all the same baggage" as their fathers. The subject is one Bruce has never shied away from (see pg. 140), but his wise words in 2021 reveal the deeper understanding he's gained over the years. Admitting he was in his 30s before he realized he might be doomed to repeat his family history, Bruce told Obama about dismantling his own baggage to avoid passing it on.

Though it never truly vanishes, pain doesn't have to haunt you forever. You can always reshape it and learn to use it to your advantage.

Bruce backstage at the
then-1st Mariner Arena
in Baltimore, Maryland,
on November 20, 2009.

"The past is never the past.
It is always present.
And you better reckon with
it in your life and in
your daily experience,
or it will get you.
It will get you really bad."

THE OBSERVER MUSIC MONTHLY, JANUARY 2009

Bruce poses for renowned music photographer David Gahr on a Jersey Shore street in August 1973.

PROVE IT ALL NIGHT

Having a "boulder on [your] shoulder," as Bruce puts it in "Blinded by the Light," can be a motivating factor when chasing dreams.

N A STORY from *Springsteen on Broadway*, the Boss talks about one of the first real shots he and one of his early bar bands had at proving their prowess. One night at a venue called the Student Prince in Asbury Park, Bruce's girlfriend at the time brought a successful music industry contact to scope out the band for a potential recording deal. "We played for this guy like we were at Madison Square Garden, everything we had, all night long," Bruce tells the crowd. Despite wowing the bigwig with his limitless skill and stamina, though, the young singer didn't get the result he was looking for: "Then he slept with my girlfriend and left town."

While any other starving artist may have been too crushed to continue

Bruce on stage at Hampden Park in Glasgow, Scotland, on June 18, 2013

chasing their dream, Bruce was not about to be deterred by such a gut punch. The Boss was as hungry as they come, and at that point, he likely had even more motivation to make a name for himself. When he finally got another major opportunity—this time a Columbia Records label audition—he was homeless, spending most nights in a sleeping bag on a friend's floor. He walked into Columbia's offices with nothing to lose and everything to gain; when producer John Hammond told him, "Look, just play me something," Bruce picked up his guitar and fired off "It's Hard to Be a Saint in the City." As soon as he finished the song, the young songwriter was told he'd earned himself a record deal.

Today, Bruce continues to prove you don't even have to be young to be hungry. In 2022, when asked by Howard Stern if he'd ever retire, he replied, "Nah, I can't imagine it," adding he'd have to be "incapacitated." Many folks do their best work when they feel the phantom weight of a chip on their shoulder. As long as you don't let it weigh you down, the feeling of having something to prove can keep your fire burning for as long as you're willing to make it happen.

Bruce carries a camera at his home in Colts Neck, New Jersey, on September 26, 2019.

OFF THE CLOCK, YOU'RE THE BOSS

"When I'm out in the street, I walk the way I wanna walk
When I'm out in the street, I talk the way I wanna talk"

"OUT IN THE STREET"

A STRONG WORK ETHIC is something to be admired, but Bruce has long shown us it's entirely possible to have both an incredible career and a happy home life (see pg. 28). Despite being one of the most prolific songwriters in rock & roll history, the Boss isn't penning new tunes as tirelessly as one might expect. In fact, the singer told Howard Stern in 2022 he often goes months without even attempting to write a song, preferring to let his work happen naturally rather than forcing it. "I have a few hobbies," he told the Sirius XM radio host, revealing he enjoys the time he spends away from making music. "My sister's a terrific photographer, Pam Springsteen, and so she's gotten me into taking some pictures. So I'll do some photography just for fun."

The mental and physical energy it takes to be good at your job can leave you exhausted. When you're off the clock and there's no need to burn that fuel, don't be afraid to follow your most leisurely whims. Everyone needs some time "out in the street" to focus on their own idea of fun.

Bruce waves to fans at the Tribeca Film Festival in New York City on April 28, 2017.

Bruce talks to the media following a sound check at Perth Arena in Perth, Australia, on January 22, 2017.

CONTAIN MULTITUDES

Bruce's ability to bounce between a limitless dynamo on stage and a humble, soft speaker in interviews shows there's no need to feel tied to one distinct identity.

THE BOSS HAS long been an advocate for "keep[ing] two completely contradictory ideas alive and well inside of your heart and head at all times" (see pg. 86). While this may sound like a challenging philosophy, Bruce has been doing it effortlessly for as long as he's been in the public eye. The man, like his music, is proof that it pays to be dynamic.

If you were to attend an E Street Band concert, you'd see the Boss, a living legend who knows just how good he is, reveling in adulation and giving his all to the audience until he's soaked to the bone. But then you could turn on the TV the next night and see Bruce sitting on the couch of a late-night talk show, humbly laughing off the host's

The Boss performs at the Asbury Park Convention Hall on March 23, 2009.

praise and answering questions with a surprising shyness. While it's well-documented that the man commanding the crowds at his shows is partially a persona, that's still the person Bruce is compelled to be whenever he steps on stage. Similarly, the singer follows his instinct to be his truest self for promotional appearances, opting not to "perform" as some celebrities do. It's easy to see how introverts and extroverts alike could see themselves represented by Bruce.

On *Renegades: Born in the USA*, the podcast he cohosted with Barack Obama, Bruce discussed the different versions of his personality the public has gotten to know over time. "What's more domineering than coming out in front of a stadium in front of 50,000 people?" the Boss said. "It's gladiatorial." He said this while putting that very duality on display, trading the roaring audience and the thumping drums for a candid, tear-jerking conversation with a friend.

It's natural to want to highlight some of your character traits while hiding others. Be like Bruce—embrace all the (harmless) aspects of your personality. They'll make you a more complete picture.

E Street Band members Clarence Clemons, Bruce Springsteen, Garry Tallent and Steven Van Zandt perform in an undated photo.

"Finding that center,
finding that purpose,
finding out who you want to be,
the story you want to tell—
that's deeply essential
to a happy life."

RTL NEDERLAND INTERVIEW WITH HUMBERTO TAN

Bruce Springsteen &
the E Street Band pose
for a photo c. 1977.

IF IT AIN'T BROKE, DON'T FIX IT...

With a career 21 studio albums and 50 years on, Bruce has shown that a solid foundation will allow you to stand the test of time.

B RUCE SPRINGSTEEN'S BODY of work remains as relevant as ever today thanks to a factor only the greatest artists manage to achieve: timelessness. Sure, most folks today don't know what it's like to get behind the wheel of a '69 Chevy, but a song like "Racing in the Street" is still just as evocative. From the subjects he's written about to the guitar he's played to the clothes he's worn, very little has changed over the years when it comes to the Boss's presentation. And with the success he's seen, why should it?

On a 2020 appearance on *The Tonight Show Starring Jimmy Fallon*, Bruce talked about the many lessons he learned performing with his very first band and how they've continued to hold true with the E Street

Bruce plays his Fender Telecaster in a performance with the E Street Band in October 1985.

Band, with whom he's been playing for roughly half a century. The Elks Club in Freehold, New Jersey, held the first stage he ever stepped onto in pursuit of his rock & roll dreams, and it was there that he began a tradition he continues to this day. "I got up and sang 'Twist and Shout,' and I've been singing it ever since," Bruce told Fallon.

Not only has the Boss been delighting crowds with a favorite cover for the entire duration of his performing career, he's also been playing the same guitar for the majority of that time. Bruce's "mutt" Fender Telecaster—seen on the iconic cover of his album *Born to Run*—has been "in every club, theater, arena and stadium across America and most of the world," as the singer told Stephen Colbert during a 2021 appearance on *The Late Show*. "This became an extension of my actual body," Bruce said. "Anything else I pick up, it's [just] a guitar."

Many artists feel the only way to keep up with the times is to make big changes to themselves. But Bruce continues to stand tall while still donning leather jackets and jeans and singing about many of the same struggles he always has. Don't feel pressured by outside forces to change something you like about yourself. If it works for you and you enjoy it, keep it intact.

BRUCE SPRINGSTEEN

NEBRASKA

A vinyl record of Bruce's 1982 album *Nebraska*.

...BUT SHAKE THINGS UP ONCE IN A WHILE

Bruce's off-the-beaten-path records are inspiring examples of what can happen when you step outside your comfort zone.

THE SIGNATURE SOUND of Bruce Springsteen is hallmarked by guitar chords that rumble like thunder, piano and glockenspiel arrangements that prance like summer rain and saxophone solos that arrive like a much-needed breeze. For half a century, the Boss's ability to stick to his foundational elements has served him very well (see pg. 124), but that's thanks, in part, to his willingness to shake up his sound every now and again.

In 1982, with five albums to his name already cementing his place in rock & roll history, Bruce decided to show the world his quieter side. Intending to merely record demos for what would be the next E Street Band album, the singer ended up making what's now one of his most beloved classics, *Nebraska*. The Boss's decision to leave the songs in their original form as raw acoustic sketches opened the eyes (and ears)

Bruce performs in the 2019 *Western Stars* documentary.

of many—if there were ever any doubt Bruce could have just as easily made it as a pure folk artist, this album put it to rest.

In the decades since *Nebraska*, the Boss hasn't let his senior citizenship stop him from experimenting. While other elder statesmen of rock might use their age as an excuse to recycle old recipes to make more albums, Bruce continues to explore new frontiers, with 2019's *Western Stars* serving as a prime example. Accompanied by pedal steel, banjo and an assortment of brass instruments, the rock legend pleasantly surprised longtime listeners with, as a *Rolling Stone* review put it, "country-tinged California pop from the '60s and '70s, sounding like nothing he's done before." A few years later, in 2022, the Boss would again opt to go against the grain, this time releasing an album of classic soul covers called *Only the Strong Survive*. When performing singles from the album on late-night talk shows, he swapped his usual stage aesthetic for sharp suits and set aside his guitar to put all the focus on his impressive pipes.

It can be tough to break out of your comfort zone, especially if it's serving you well. But when you dare to try something new once in a while, it can help that old hat feel fresh again.

Bruce in the 2019 *Western Stars* documentary.

AN OPEN MIND OPENS DOORS

The Boss's willingness to say "yes" reveals
how rewarding receptiveness can be.

K NOWING HOW TO navigate opportunities and choose what's best for you is a skill that continues to develop throughout life. But one surefire way to stunt that development is by saying "no" to anything that seems outside your wheelhouse. Bruce, on the contrary, continues to show what good can come from constantly keeping an open mind.

On a 2022 appearance on *The Graham Norton Show*, the Boss told the story of one of the most meaningful fan interactions he's ever had. In the 1980s, when his star status was ascending to incredible heights, Bruce spent a night off at a movie theater in St. Louis, where he was unsurprisingly spotted by a fan. "I met a kid in the lobby there with his girlfriend who said, 'Do you wanna sit with us?'" Bruce recalled. "So I said, 'OK.'" After his bold invitation paid off, the young fan decided to try his luck again and test Bruce's openness even further. "Will you

come home and meet my parents?" the singer remembered being asked after the movie, to which he replied with another nonchalant, "OK." "So around midnight I was sitting in a little house in St. Louis having some eggs with this kid and his mom," Bruce told the host before revealing the heartwarming result of accepting this unique invitation: "And I saw them for decades after that every time we came to town."

In recent years, the Boss's open mind has also yielded dream-come-true collaborations for several artists. While some legends may feel no need to brush shoulders with the young music makers of today, Bruce embraces those who are changing the landscape of the industry. Jack Antonoff—renowned pop producer for the likes of Lorde, Lana Del Ray and Carly Rae Jepsen—is one such massive Boss fan. Antonoff, who records as the band Bleachers, got to work with the man himself on Bleachers' 2020 single "Chinatown." And thanks to the friendship he developed with Antonoff, Bruce is also open to teaming up with one of Antonoff's most prolific professional partners: Taylor Swift. When asked by Jimmy Fallon in 2022 if that would ever happen, the Boss said, "She's welcome on E Street anytime." When the occasional odd opportunity comes knocking, don't be afraid to answer the door.

Jessica Springsteen, Sam Springsteen, Patti Scialfa, Bruce and Evan Springsteen backstage at the Eugene O'Neill Theater on August 8, 2008, in New York City.

"Children bring with them grace, patience, transcendence, second chances, rebirth and a reawakening of the love that's in your heart and present in your home. They are God giving you another shot."

BORN TO RUN (2016 AUTOBIOGRAPHY)

Bruce dances with his mother, Adele Springsteen, during the Hard Rock Calling Festival at Olympic Park in London on June 30, 2013.

PARENTS ARE A BLUEPRINT (FOR BETTER OR WORSE)

Bruce became the man he is by understanding the brightest traits and darkest shadows exhibited by his parents.

F ROM CELEBRATING HIS mother's warmth in "The Wish" to addressing his father's cold ways in "My Father's House," Bruce has always been open about both the good and the bad of his upbringing. "We honor our parents by carrying their best forward and laying the rest down," he wrote in his autobiography *Born to Run*. "By fighting and taming the demons that laid them low and now reside in us."

On an episode of their podcast *Renegades: Born in the USA*, the Boss and Barack Obama discussed how their fathers' traits can be traced back generations. "He was an unknowable man," Bruce said of Douglas Springsteen. "I have to believe he got this from his father. And the only thing I knew about my grandfather was he disappeared for periods of

Bruce performs in Netflix's
Springsteen on Broadway
special (2018).

time. And my father carried on that secrecy." While his father may not have been able to recognize the "demons" he'd inherited, Bruce was able—and it gave him the chance to break the cycle: "It was something that was handed down that I had to work hard not to emulate."

Still, when it came to his career, Bruce did emulate his father in many ways. "I think I created my particular stage persona out of my dad's life and perhaps I even built it to suit him to some degree," the singer told NPR in 2016. From the clothing he wore on stage to the muscle he gained to the numerous songs about working class struggles, Bruce was well into his 30s before he even realized he was drawing so much from the man he frequently clashed with growing up. The reason for this, as he told Obama on *Renegades*, was an attempt to rewrite the relationship: "When you can't get the love you want from the parent you want it from, how do you get the intimacy you need? I can't get to him, and I can't have him...I'll be him. That's what I'll do, I'll be him."

By bringing us into the world, parents give us their greatest gifts and their heaviest baggage. Don't simply embrace the former and disregard the latter—both can be equally valuable for figuring out exactly who you are.

LOVE CAN TEACH YOU A LOT

"I don't think I got to where I wanted to be as a man until Patti was in my life. [She] schooled me on some serious things I needed schooling on."

RENEGADES: BORN IN THE USA PODCAST

WHEN BRUCE MET "the queen of [his] heart," Patti Scialfa, he was still picking up the pieces from his previous marriage to see what went wrong. And once the two began their relationship, the singer recognized just how much wisdom he stood to gain from the new apple of his eye. One crucial lesson he learned? The fact that he still had a lot to learn. "To learn the skills of loving, which are real, I didn't understand 'Oh, I've gotta work on this like I worked on the guitar,'" Bruce told Howard Stern in 2022.

The learning hasn't stopped since the duo wed in 1991, as the Boss has recently credited Patti with helping him reach realizations ranging from the joys of being an early bird to the ways in which he should deal with his depression. Honing the elusive "skills of loving" can take a while. Don't get discouraged—do as Bruce suggested while discussing the subject with Stern: "Put your mind there and hope that your ass will follow!"

Bruce and Patti Scialfa arrive at a Rock & Roll Hall of Fame dinner at the Waldorf Astoria in New York City on January 17, 1991.

THE UNIVERSE SENDS YOU SIGNS

**As Bruce can attest, sometimes the answers to life's big questions
are right in front of you—you just have to pay attention.**

FROM NAMING HIS 2007 album after the concept to discussing the secret sorcery behind his songwriting (see pg. 18), Bruce has always operated with the help of a little "magic." And it's easy to see why the Boss occasionally welcomes the idea that some things can't be explained with simple logic and reason: Two of the most important people he's ever known appeared before him in undeniably fateful fashion.

During his Rock & Roll Hall of Fame induction speech in 1999, Bruce told the story of how he and Clarence Clemons found each other. As the songwriter tells it, the Big Man's presence was so thunderous, it was immediately clear he and the Boss could catch lightning in a bottle together.

Bruce and Patti
Scialfa perform in East
Rutherford, New Jersey,
on August 22, 1985.

"The night I met Clarence, he got up on stage and a sound came out his horn that seemed to rattle the glasses behind the bar and threatened to blow out the back wall," the singer began. "Then the door literally blew off the club in a storm that night, and I knew I'd found my sax player."

Fittingly, the love of Bruce's life has a similar origin story. While hanging out at the Stone Pony in Asbury Park one night in 1984, the Boss was smitten with the mysterious redhead who sat in with the house band. "That is the night I fell in love with Patti's voice," he says in *Springsteen on Broadway*. As he watched her perform "Tell Him" by the Exciters, Bruce realized the universe itself might be singing to him through the voice of this woman. "The first line of the first song I ever heard Patti sing was 'I know something about love,'" he tells the audience before bringing his wife on stage, adding, "She does."

You don't have to be a big believer in fate, magic or anything of the sort to be nudged in the right direction. "Seeing signs" can just be an enchanted version of "going with your gut." But whether it's the universe or your gut that seems to be telling you something, you might wanna listen up.

The Boss during a session filmed for *Bruce Springsteen's Letter to You* (2020).

"*Some things imprint themselves on you and never let go.*"

BRUCE SPRINGSTEEN'S *LETTER TO YOU* DOCUMENTARY

Nils Lofgren, Bruce and Steven Van Zandt perform in Los Angeles, California, on March 15, 2016.

AGE EQUALS WISDOM AND EXPERIENCE

"You can't be afraid of getting old. Old is good if you're gathering in life. Our band is good at understanding that equation."

CLASH MAGAZINE, 2010

WHILE NOT EVERYONE can age as gracefully as Bruce Springsteen on the outside, anyone can learn to accept the inevitability of time as well as the Boss has. As natural as it is to cling to your youth, you might eventually see your younger years as a different life altogether. Touching on the subject in a 2020 *AARP* interview, Bruce said, "I heard something of mine from 1975 on a record the other day and I said, 'That was about seven or eight lives ago.'"

With all those past lives under his belt, Bruce has earned his position as a source of spiritual guidance for fans all over the world. And when he combines his experience with that of the E Street Band, together they form a force fueled by decades of absorbed wisdom about both music and life in general. You're going to get old—the best thing you can do is embrace it and revel in everything your accumulated time has given you.

A vinyl record of Bruce's 2002 album *The Rising*.

INSPIRE STRENGTH IN OTHERS

**Whenever his fans have needed the healing effects of his music,
Bruce has answered the call.**

N A PROFILE for the October/November 2020 issue of *AARP*, editor-in-chief Robert Love dubbed Bruce Springsteen "the great empath of the rock world," noting, "He shows up for causes big and small: hunger, poverty, Vietnam vets, 9/11 first responders, hurricane relief and many more, right down to Asbury Park local." The Boss has always preached the importance of lending a helping hand, as he, on many occasions, has admitted to being the one searching for strength. When you know what it's like to need and then receive that support, it's easy to reciprocate.

The aftermath of September 11, 2001, was a time in which Americans everywhere were in dire need of hope and strength. As Bruce watched in horror as the second plane hit the south tower of the World Trade Center on live TV that day, he was in the early stages of writing and recording his 12th studio album—which would come to be forever tied to the tragic events. Shortly after the attacks, the songwriter headed to the beach below a coastal bridge in New Jersey to reckon with this horrendous reality when a

stranger pulled up beside him, rolled down the window and said, "We need you now." Less than a year later, Bruce and the E Street Band delivered *The Rising*, an album that spoke to the feelings that lingered in the wake of 9/11. In the cathartic title track, Bruce comes through with the sense of hope asked of him by that stranger in the car, inviting the listener to "Come on up, lay your hands in mine." And though he originally wrote the track "My City of Ruins" about Asbury Park, it was clear the Boss was providing a prayer for strength to mourning New Yorkers when he performed the song during the *America: A Tribute to Heroes* benefit.

In 2020, when the world needed some light at the end of the tunnel due to the COVID-19 pandemic, Bruce again rose to the occasion. This time, the Boss took to the airwaves in the form of a Sirius XM radio show called *From My Home to Yours*, during which he lifted the spirits of listeners with the simple statement "Stay strong, stay home and stay together." By broadcasting from his home—where he, like everyone else, was stuck—the singer provided a sense of comfort and unity.

You don't have to be a beloved rock icon to inspire strength in others. Simply reminding them they're not alone is often the key to providing that power.

Bruce performs during the Born in the U.S.A. tour, October 1985.

WE'RE ALL IN THIS TOGETHER

"Nobody wins unless everybody wins."

BORN IN THE U.S.A. TOUR, 1984-85

I N THE MID-1980s, as *Born in the U.S.A.* was bursting out of boomboxes like 4th of July fireworks and the Reagan administration had many folks feeling left behind, Bruce began concluding his live shows with the powerful statement above. While encapsulating what it means to exist as a united state, the notion also resonated beyond American borders, where a British-Pakistani Muslim teenager named Sarfraz Manzoor was wielding the music of Bruce Springsteen like a weapon against discrimination. Manzoor's story later inspired the 2019 film *Blinded by the Light*, in which the protagonist Javed (Viveik Kalra), a victim of constant racism in Luton, England, is encouraged by the messages in Bruce's music to pursue a writing career despite being rejected by his school newspaper. In one scene, Javed utters Bruce's "Nobody wins..." phrase, bringing the inspirational tale full circle. But whether you're living in 1987 Britain or modern America, the same will always be true: Victory isn't so sweet when it comes at someone else's expense. Real triumph is standing tall beside your fellow man.

Bruce poses for a
photo shoot c. 1978.

"Some folks are born
into a good life
And other folks get it
any way, any how."

"DARKNESS ON THE EDGE OF TOWN"

• • •

In the title track of his 1978 album *Darkness on the Edge of Town*,
Bruce highlights a classic socioeconomic clash: those who coast on the good
fortune they've had since day one versus those who tirelessly hustle to earn
their keep. But thanks to their struggles, the latter group tend to be the
ones who truly understand what it means to have a "good life."

Clarence Clemons and Bruce bring the house down on a tour stop in 1978.

NO ONE IS EVER TRULY GONE

**As Bruce says, "Everything dies, baby, that's a fact."
But the Boss has shown time and again that if you keep the
memories alive through song, celebration or any other means,
the people you've lost can remain prominent in your life.**

N 2011, WHEN the world lost Clarence Clemons, the E Street Band's towering, magnetic saxophonist, Bruce eulogized his dear friend as only he could: "How big was the Big Man?" the Boss asked attendees at Clarence's funeral. "Too fucking big to die," he answered. For fans, this statement is an irrefutable fact. Anytime the band hits the road, they're now joined by the Big Man's own blood as his nephew Jake Clemons mans the mighty horn that will forever be essential to the E Street sound. When Bruce reaches the line in "Tenth Avenue Freeze Out" recalling when "the Big Man joined the band," the music stops as the screens surrounding the stage roll classic footage of Bruce and Clarence setting the world ablaze. In that moment, Clarence's presence fills the

Jake Clemons and Bruce perform at Climate Pledge Arena in Seattle, Washington, on February 27, 2023.

arena in a capacity that redefines the phrase "larger than life."

On his 2020 album *Letter to You*, Bruce continues to celebrate the legacies of those he's lost over the years. In the accompanying documentary film, the Boss honors the memories of Clarence Clemons and the E Street Band's late keyboardist Danny Federici, but he also calls attention to the loss of friends from one of his first bands, the Castiles. In a poignant moment before the song "Last Man Standing," Bruce reveals he's the only surviving member of that group. But in the closing track on *Letter to You*, the Boss finds (and provides) comfort with a simple sentiment: "I'll see you in my dreams."

Losing loved ones is something we all have to face as time goes on. But you can keep someone's spirit alive if you honor the way they lived and cherish the connection you shared. This philosophy isn't unique to Bruce, though it's one he feels confident enough about to proselytize to others. In a 2021 appearance on *The Late Show with Stephen Colbert*, when the host asked him what happens when we die, the Boss said "Individual consciousness? Adios. But our souls and our spirits I think live on with the people we've loved and who've loved us." Maybe everything that dies really does come back someday.

The E Street Band: Danny Federici, Clarence Clemons, Max Weinberg, Bruce, Steven Van Zandt, Roy Bittan and Garry Tallent in Red Bank, New Jersey, on October 17, 1979.

TWO HEARTS ARE BETTER THAN ONE

Even before his name was known beyond the confines of Asbury Park, New Jersey, Bruce has been preaching (and proving) that there's strength in numbers.

D ESPITE *SPRINGSTEEN ON Broadway* technically falling under the "one-man show" umbrella, its stories are populated with the people who made Bruce the man he is today: his parents, his bandmates, his wife and his many friends and fans. The Boss has always been a firm believer in collectivism, recognizing that there have been many unseen hands helping him succeed throughout his life and career. In 2022, while telling Howard Stern about the families in Freehold who would open their homes so his bands could have a place to practice for hours on end, Bruce asserted, "These are the unsung heroes of rock & roll. These are the people who form the support network that gets you to the point before you ever see a record company or make a record. They help you survive till then."

Bruce made sure to emphasize this philosophy when he was inducted into the Rock & Roll Hall of Fame in 1999, giving a nearly 17-minute

Bruce and producer Jon Landau with members of the E Street Band during a session at the Power Station recording studio in New York City, March 1980.

speech in which he sang the praises of everyone who helped him achieve the incredible honor. When he got to Clarence Clemons, the Boss expressed deep appreciation for the ways in which their partnership transcended the music they made. "Together we told the story of the possibilities of friendship," Bruce said of his legendary companionship with the Big Man. "A story older than the ones I was writing, and a story I could never have told without him at my side." And when the E Street Band got their own Rock & Roll Hall of Fame induction in 2014, their fearless leader revisited this concept, putting the spotlight on the people around him rather than himself. In his speech, Bruce honored the men and women he's shared the stage with for so many years, saying, "The hallmark of a rock & roll band is that the narrative you tell together is bigger than any you could have told on your own."

While accomplishing something all on your own is certainly admirable, it's not always possible. There's no shame in needing someone standing beside you on your journey to greatness, or lending you a hand when you're down on your luck. Whatever you're up against, don't feel like you have to go it alone—even if that means simply putting on a Bruce Springsteen record.

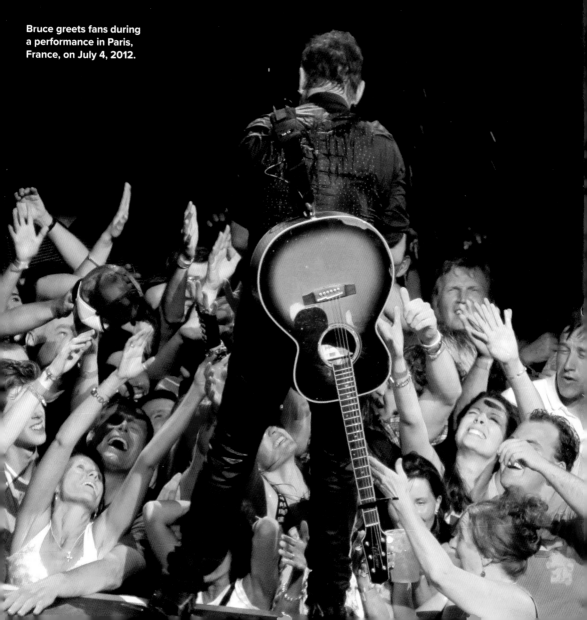

Bruce greets fans during a performance in Paris, France, on July 4, 2012.

"People don't come to
rock shows to learn something.
They come to be reminded
of something they already
know and feel

deep down in their gut."

BORN TO RUN (2016 AUTOBIOGRAPHY)

PHOTOGRAPHY CREDITS

COVER: RICHARD E. AARON/REDFERNS/GETTY IMAGES. DIGITAL IMAGING BY ERIC HEINTZ
BACK COVER: ROBIN TAKUMI/ALAMY

2 Taylor Hill/Getty Images; 4 Tom Hill/WireImage/Getty Images; 6 Tom Hill/WireImage/Getty Images; 8 Scott Kowalchyk/ CBS via Getty Images; 10 Gary Gershoff/Getty Images; 12 Bob Riha, Jr./Getty Images; 14 Joe Papeo/Shutterstock; 16 Bill Uhrich/MediaNews Group/Reading Eagle via Getty Images; 18 Bruce Glikas/FilmMagic/Getty Images; 20 Kevin Mazur/ Getty Images; 22 Rick Diamond/Getty Images; 24 Chris Walter/WireImage/Getty Images; 26 Bobby Bank/WireImage/Getty Images; 28 Tom Stoddart/Getty Images; 30 Hulton Archive/Getty Images; 32 Vinyls/Alamy; 34 Paul Natkin/WireImage/Getty Images; 36 Ron Galella, Ltd./Ron Galella Collection via Getty Images; 38 Charles Bertram/Lexington Herald-Leader/Tribune News Service via Getty Images; 40 David Tan/Shinko Music/Getty Images; 42 Kevin Kane/Getty Images for HBO; 44 TCD/ Prod.DB/Alamy; 46 KMazur/WireImage for Shore Fire Media/Getty Images; 48 Justin Sullivan/Getty Images; 50 SGranitz/ WireImage/Getty Images; 52 Andrew Harnik/AP/Shutterstock; 54 Vinyls/Alamy; 56 Theo Wargo/Getty Images for Tribeca Film Festival; 58 Vinyls/Alamy; 60 Michael Williamson/The Washington Post via Getty Images; 62 Allan Tannenbaum/Getty Images; 64 Records/Alamy; 66 Jason Reed/Reuters/Alamy; 68 Pictorial Press Ltd/Alamy; 70 Paul Natkin/Getty Images; 72 Michelangeloop/Dreamstime; 74 Tom Hill/WireImage/Getty Images; 76 Harry Durrant/Getty Images; 78 Allan Tannenbaum/ Getty Images; 80 Geoffrey Robinson/Shutterstock; 82 The Cover Version/Alamy; 84 Jersey 4 Jersey/Getty Images for ABA; 86 Michael Buckner/Getty Images for SXSW; 88 Joe Papeo/Shutterstock; 90 Jim Forbes/Corbis/VCG via Getty Images; 92 Richard E. Aaron/Redferns/Getty Images; 94 Wally Skalij/Los Angeles Times via Getty Images; 96 Taylor Hill/Getty Images; 98 George Rose/Getty Images; 100 Wally Skalij/Los Angeles Times via Getty Images; 102 Rick Diamond/Getty Images; 104 Michael S. Williamson/The Washington Post/Getty Images; 106 Joe Raedle/Getty Images; 108 Michael S. Williamson/The Washington Post/Getty Images; 110 David Gahr/Getty Images; 112 Ross Gilmore/Redferns via Getty Images; 114 Michael S. Williamson/The Washington Post/Getty Images; 116 Kevin Mazur/Gettty Images for Tribeca Film Festival; 118 Paul Kane/Getty Images; 120 Wally Skalij/Los Angeles Times via Getty Images; 122 Lynn Goldsmith/Corbis/VCG via Getty Images; 124 Archive PL/Alamy; 126 Pictorial Press Ltd/Alamy; 128 Michelangeloop/Dreamstime; 130 TCD/Prod.DB/Alamy; 132 TCD/ Prod.DB/Alamy; 134 David Gahr/Getty Images; 136 Steve Rapport/Getty Images; 138 Bruce Glikas/FilmMagic/Getty Images; 140 Geoffrey Robinson/Shutterstock; 142 PictureLux/The Hollywood Archive/Alamy; 144 Chris Walter/WireImage/Getty Images; 146 Robin Platzer/Getty Images; 148 Michael Putland/Getty Images; 150 Gary Gershoff/Getty Images; 152 Apple TV+/Everett Collection; 154 Kevin Winter/Getty Images; 156 Kate Melvin for Topix Media Lab; 158 KMazur/WireImage/Getty Images; 160 Pictorial Press Ltd/Alamy; 162 Michael Ochs Archives/Getty Images; 164 Michael Putland/Getty Images; 166 Mat Hayward/Getty Images; 168 David Gahr/Getty Images; 170 David Gahr/Getty Images; 172 Geoffrey Robinson/Shutterstock

TREVOR COURNEEN is a writer, editor and Bruce Springsteen fanatic whose credits include various music features and reviews for *Paste* as well as special projects for *Time Life* and *Newsweek*, including in memoriam magazines for Prince and George Michael. When he isn't penning works for Media Lab Books, he enjoys playing with his band Deep Wimp and trying to channel the Boss's energy as much as possible. He and his wife live in Brooklyn.

Media Lab Books
For inquiries, call 646-449-8614

Copyright 2023 Topix Media Lab

Published by Topix Media Lab
14 Wall Street, Suite 3C
New York, NY 10005

Printed in China

ISBN-13: 978-1-956403-42-8
ISBN-10: 1-956403-42-6